A Note to Parents and Teachers

Kids can imagine, kids can laugh and kids can learn to read with this exciting new series of first readers. Each book in the Kids Can Read series has been especially written, illustrated and designed for beginning readers. Humorous, easy-to-read stories, appealing characters, and engaging illustrations make for books that kids will want to read over and over again.

To make selecting a book easy for kids, parents and teachers, the Kids Can Read series offers three levels based on different reading abilities:

Level 1: Kids Can Start to Read

Short stories, simple sentences, easy vocabulary, lots of repetition and visual clues for kids just beginning to read.

Level 2: Kids Can Read with Help

Longer stories, varied sentences, increased vocabulary, some repetition and visual clues for kids who have some reading skills, but may need a little help.

Level 3: Kids Can Read Alone

Longer, more complex stories and sentences, more challenging vocabulary, language play, minimal repetition and visual clues for kids who are reading by themselves.

With the Kids Can Read series, kids can enter a new and exciting world of reading!

Franklin's Surprise

From an episode of the animated TV series *Franklin*, produced by Nelvana Limited, Neurones France s.a.r.l. and Neurones Luxembourg S.A., based on the Franklin books by Paulette Bourgeois and Brenda Clark.

Story written by Sharon Jennings.

Illustrated by Sean Jeffrey, Mark Koren and Alice Sinkner.

Based on the TV episode *Franklin's Party Plan*, written by Betty Quan.

™ Kids Can Read is a trademark of Kids Can Press Ltd.

Franklin is a trademark of Kids Can Press Ltd.
The character Franklin was created by Paulette Bourgeois and Brenda Clark.
Text © 2003 Contextx Inc.
Illustrations © 2003 Brenda Clark Illustrator Inc.

Kids Can Press acknowledges the financial support of the Ontario Arts Council, the Canada Council for the Arts and the Government of Canada, through the BPIDP, for our publishing activity.

Published in Canada by
Kids Can Press Ltd.
29 Birch Avenue
Toronto, ON M4V 1E2

Published in the U.S. by
Kids Can Press Ltd.
2250 Military Road
Tonawanda, NY 14150

www.kidscanpress.com

Series editor: Tara Walker
Edited by David MacDonald and Yvette Ghione

Printed in Hong Kong, China, by Wing King Tong Company Limited

The hardcover edition of this book is smyth sewn casebound.
The paperback edition of this book is limp sewn with a drawn-on cover.

CM 03 0 9 8 7 6 5 4 3 2 1
CM PA 03 0 9 8 7 6 5 4 3 2 1

National Library of Canada Cataloguing in Publication Data

Jennings, Sharon
    Franklin's Surprise / Sharon Jennings ; illustrated by Sean Jeffrey, Mark Koren, Alice Sinkner.

(Kids Can read)
The character Franklin was created by Paulette Bourgeois and Brenda Clark.

ISBN 1-55337-465-7 (bound).   ISBN 1-55337-466-5 (pbk.)

I. Jeffrey, Sean II. Koren, Mark III. Sinkner, Alice IV. Bourgeois, Paulette
V. Clark, Brenda VI. Title. VII. Series: Kids Can read (Toronto, Ont.)

PS8569.E563F778 2003   jC813'.54   C2003-901302-2
PZ7

Kids Can Press is a ℃o**rus** ™ Entertainment company

Franklin's Surprise

Kids Can Press

Franklin can tie his shoes.

Franklin can count by twos.

He can also plan

a super surprise party.

When Franklin plans a surprise party,

even Franklin gets surprised.

One day, Franklin was riding his bicycle.

He rode by Skunk's house.

He saw a sign on the lawn.

The sign said "SOLD."

"Oh, no!" cried Franklin.

Franklin jumped off his bicycle.

He ran up to Skunk's door.

8

BANG! BANG! BANG!

banged Franklin.

But no one came.

"This is terrible!"
said Franklin.
"Skunk did not tell me
she was moving."

Franklin got back on his bicycle.

He rode by his house.

"Skunk is moving," he called

to his mother.

"I know," she said. "But —"

Franklin kept going.

"I have to tell everybody!" he shouted.

Franklin found his friends at the park.

He told them the terrible news.

12

"I'll miss Skunk,"

said Beaver.

"Me too,"

said Bear.

"Me too," said everybody else.

Franklin had

an idea.

"Let's have a going-away party

for Skunk," he said.

"It will be a surprise."

"Hooray!" said everybody.

"Come to my house this afternoon," said Franklin.

"I'll bring ice cream," said Bear.

"I'll bring cookies," said Beaver.

"We'll bring candy," said everybody else.

Franklin rode home.

"We are having a going-away party

for Skunk," he told his mother.

"It will be a big surprise."

"It sure will," said his mother. "But —"

Franklin ran to his room.

"I have lots to do," he said.

Franklin blew up
lots of balloons.

Then he baked a cake.
"I wrote 'Goodbye Skunk' on the cake,"
he told his mother.
"But Franklin—"
she began.

Just then, Franklin looked

out the window.

Skunk was coming up the walk.

"Oh, no!" cried Franklin.

"What is Skunk doing here?"

Franklin ran to his room.

His mother came to find him.

"Skunk has something to tell you,"
she said.

20

"I don't want to see Skunk

until the party," Franklin whispered.

"I might give away the surprise."

"But Franklin —" began his mother.

"Shhh!"

said Franklin.

When Skunk was gone,

Franklin called his friends.

They came over and hung

balloons and streamers.

Franklin put up a sign that said

"Goodbye Skunk."

Goodbye Skunk

"This is a good party," said Bear.

"You thought of everything."

"Thank you,"

said Franklin.

"Where is Skunk?"

asked Beaver.

"Oops!" said Franklin.

"I didn't think of that."

Just then, Franklin looked

out the window.

Skunk was coming back.

"Everybody hide!" Franklin cried.

Everybody hid.

Franklin opened the door.

"SURPRISE!" everybody shouted.

Skunk was very surprised.

Franklin showed Skunk

the sign that said "Goodbye Skunk."

He showed her the cake

that said "Goodbye Skunk."

"Goodbye, Skunk," said Franklin.

"We will miss you."

"But Franklin—" said Skunk.

"Please write to us," said Franklin.

"But Franklin—" said Skunk.

"Have some cake," said Franklin.

"FRANKLIN!" shouted Skunk.

"I HAVE SOMETHING TO TELL YOU!"

Everybody looked at Skunk.

"Follow me," she said.

Everybody followed Skunk.

They went to the house across the lane.

Skunk went inside and shut the door.

Then she opened the door.

"SURPRISE!" she shouted.

"This is my new house."

Everybody looked at Franklin.

"HOORAY!" shouted Franklin.

"Let's go to my house

and have a not-going-away party."

Everybody went to Franklin's house.

And ...

SURPRISE!

It was a super party, after all.